THOSE ARE NOT MY UNDERPANTS!

WITHDRAWN

by
Melissa Martin

illustrated by
Troy Cummings

Random House 🏠 New York

One fine morning, Bear Cub ambled out of his cave and stretched. Right over his head, he saw a pair of underpants hanging on a tree limb.

"Someone lost their underpants," he said. "I wonder who!" He looked them over. No name. No tag.

Bear Cub wanted to find who belonged to the underpants.
So he set off through the forest.

"Hi, Squirrel. Are these your underpants?"

"No," answered Squirrel. "Those are not my underpants."

"Are you sure?" asked Bear Cub.

"Yes. There's no hole for my tail."

"Hi, Turtle. Are these your underpants?"

"No," answered Turtle. "Those are not my underpants."

"Are you sure?" asked Bear Cub.

"Yes. I keep my underpants under my shell."

"Hi, Owl. Are these your underpants?"

"No," answered Owl. "Those are not my underpants."

"Are you sure?" asked Bear Cub.

"Yes. Owl underpants are sparkly."

"Hi, Salmon. Are these your underpants?"

"No," answered Salmon. "Those are not my underpants."

"Are you sure?" asked Bear Cub.

"Yes. Salmon don't wear underpants. We wear swimsuits."

"Hi, Bat. Are these your underpants?"

"No," answered Bat. "Those are not my underpants."

"Are you sure?" asked Bear Cub.

"Yes. Bat underpants glow in the dark."

"Hi, Skunk. Are these your underpants?"

"No," answered Skunk. "Those are not my underpants."

"Are you sure?" asked Bear Cub.

"Yes. They smell too good to be *my* underpants."

"Hi, Snake. Are these your underpants?"

"No," answered Snake. "Those are not my underpants."

"Are you sure?" asked Bear Cub.

"Yes. Snakes wear looooong underwear."

"Hi, Beaver. Are these your underpants?"

"No," answered Beaver. "Those are definitely not my underpants."

"Are you sure?" asked Bear Cub.

"Yes!" whispered Beaver. "Underpants are way too embarrassing to let everyone see them like that!"

"Hi, Moose. Are these your underpants?"

"No," answered Moose. "Those are not my underpants."

"Are you sure?" asked Bear Cub.

"Yep. Moose underpants are EXTRA LARGE!"

The underpants didn't seem to belong to anyone! So Bear Cub headed home.

"Bear Cub," asked Momma Bear, "why are you carrying your underpants around?"

"What?" he exclaimed. "These are not *my* underpants."

"But they are, honey," answered Momma Bear. "I washed them last night and hung them up to dry."

Momma Bear laughed. "You see? You're not wearing any. Those are *your* underpants."

Bear Cub looked down. "They are!" he said, laughing. "They *are* my underpants!"

He put them on. The underpants fit perfectly!

THE END